Karen, Nutte

FABLES

WEEKLY READER CHILDREN'S BOOK CLUB

INTERMEDIATE DIVISION

Aesop's Fables

WEEKLY READER CHILDRENS BOOK CLUB

presents

Aesop's Fables

Retold by Anne Terry White

Illustrated by Helen Siegl

Random House New York

To Christopher

A Word to My Readers

Animals don't talk. To be sure, we read many books in which they do. But that is just make-believe. There is no dog who can say to another dog, "You go this way, and I'll go that way, and we'll meet behind that rock."

In this book the animals talk like human beings. They feel like human beings. They act like human beings. Aesop, the clever Greek slave who told these stories, made his animals behave like that for a good reason.

His reason was that he wanted to point a moral without hurting anybody's feelings. Especially the feelings of the proud and the great, who could be very cruel to a poor slave. When he told a story about a lion, he was really telling it about the king. When he told a story about a wolf, he was really talking about some cruel nobleman. They got the point.

And we get the point too. For all of us know people who act like Aesop's lions and wolves and crows and foxes and goats and grasshoppers. In fact, we sometimes act that way ourselves.

Anne Terry White

Contents

Aesop's Fables

The Dog in the Manger

A dog one day decided to take his afternoon nap in the manger. It was warm and cozy there, and he was soon asleep.

By and by, when the day's work was done, the tired Oxen came in. The Dog woke up and started to bark at them. He stood on top of the hay and barked and barked so that the Oxen could not get near their food.

"Now aren't you a mean creature?" they said. "You cannot eat hay yourself. Yet you will not let us eat it who want it badly."

🖋 *Do not begrudge to others what you cannot use yourself.*

The Fox and the Stork

A Fox and a Stork were friends and often visited back and forth. One day the Fox invited the Stork to dinner.

"I shall be pleased to come," said the Stork. "What time?"

"Five o'clock."

Sharp at five the Stork turned up. He had smelled something good cooking from a distance and could hardly wait to begin.

"Sit right down," the Fox greeted him. And she set out the dinner. It was a fine chicken soup served in a wide shallow plate.

The Fox herself began to lap the soup up at a great rate, but the poor Stork could only wet the end of his long bill. He saw that the Fox had played a trick on him, yet he behaved as though nothing was wrong.

"Two can play at that game," he thought to himself. And when the Fox had licked the plate clean, the Stork said politely:

"Tomorrow you must come and dine with me."

At first the Fox said it would be too much trouble for her friend. Then she said it would be too costly. But at last she said:

· 4 · "What time?"

"Five o'clock."

Promptly at five o'clock the Fox arrived. But she found that the Stork knew how to play tricks too. For he had cooked a fine fish chowder but served it in a tall jar with a narrow neck.

"Help yourself," the Stork welcomed the guest. "Be at home!" And he set the example by sticking his long bill into the jar.

But all the Fox could do was lick the outside.

One trick deserves another.

The Lion and the Mouse

In the heat of the day a Lion lay asleep at the edge of a wood. He lay so still that a Mouse ran right across his nose without knowing it was a nose, and a Lion's at that.

Bang! The Lion clapped his paw to his face and felt something caught. It was furry. Lazily he opened his eyes. He lifted up one side of his huge paw just a little bit to see what was under it and was amused to find a Mouse.

.5.

"Spare me, Great King!" he heard the little creature squeak in its tiny voice. "I didn't

mean to do it! Let me go, and someday I will repay you."

"That's very funny," said the Lion, and he laughed. "How can a little thing like you help me, the great King of Beasts?"

"I don't know," the Mouse replied, "but a little creature *can* sometimes help a big one."

"Well, you have made me laugh," the Lion said, "which is something I seldom do. And anyway, you would hardly make half a mouthful. So——" He raised his paw and let the Mouse go.

A few days later the Lion was caught in a hunter's net. The woods rang with his angry roaring and the little Mouse heard him.

"That is my kind Lion!" she cried. "He is in trouble!" As fast as she could, she ran toward the spot from which the roaring came, and there he was. The Lion was thrashing around so in the net that the Mouse didn't dare to come near for fear of being crushed.

"O King, be patient!" she cried. "I will gnaw through the ropes and set you free."

So the Lion lay still while the Mouse worked

away with her sharp teeth. And in a short time he was able to creep out of the net.

"You see? I told you I would repay you," the Mouse said happily. "A little creature sometimes really can help a big one."

And the Lion had to admit it was true.

◢ *Little friends may prove to be great friends.*

The Milkmaid and Her Pail

Milkmaid Sally was on her way to market. On her pretty head she carried the pail of milk she was going to sell. And inside the pretty head she was thinking busy thoughts.

"With the money I get for my milk," she said to herself as she walked along, "I shall buy a good hen. She will lay me a whole nestful of eggs—twenty at least. But I shall not sell them. I shall let her hatch out the whole lot.

"How cute twenty little yellow chicks will be, running around the yard! I shall feed them well, and when they are of a good size, I shall

sell them. With the money I shall buy a fine new dress and a ribbon to go with it. I'll wear them to the fair. All the lads will be crazy about me. But I shall act proud and not look at one of them."

Here she tossed her pretty head to show how she would scorn the boys. And down fell the pail of milk, spilling every drop.

🖋 *Don't count your chickens before they are hatched.*

The Country Mouse and the City Mouse

"My dear, how are you?" said the Country Mouse. She kissed her cousin the City Mouse and made her welcome in her snug little hole.

"How good of you to travel all this way to visit me," she went on. "Well, you shall see how we country folk live. Not badly at all."

With that she began to carry food out of the house. The best of everything should be put on the table for her guest. They would eat outdoors in the fresh air under a tree and the birds would sing to them while they feasted.

It took a long time to carry out the moldy crust, the cheese parings, the bacon rind, and the dry peas and beans she had stored up. But all was ready at last. The dessert would be two stalks of fresh wheat which she had brought home from the field that very day. She laid them proudly on a mushroom, and very pretty they looked, too.

The Country Mouse ate heartily, but the City Mouse only nibbled at the food. She was used to better things. After the dessert she said:

"My dear, how can you bear to live in this poky way? I call this starving. You don't know what happiness is. Come with me and let me show you my way of life. You will be done with loneliness. You will live in plenty and enjoy all the pleasures your heart desires."

The Country Mouse saw nothing wrong .11.
with her way of life, but she agreed to go with her cousin and they set off at once. It was night when they reached the city.

"This is my house," the City Mouse said and led the way up the stairs and into the dining room. It was brightly lighted. On the table were the remains of a fine feast, for there had been a party that night.

"Help yourself," the City Mouse invited her cousin.

The Country Mouse scampered over the snowy cloth and stared at the dishes. She could hardly believe it wasn't all a dream. She didn't know which to taste first—the pudding, the cheese, the cakes, the jellies, or the nuts. She sniffed at the grapes and pears. They didn't look real, but yes, they were. She was very thirsty, so first of all she took a sip out of a tall, sparkling glass.

"How silly I have been to waste my life in the country," she thought. "This is heaven!"

Then she started nibbling on a piece of cake. But she had taken no more than two bites when the doors flew open. In came the servants with their friends and a couple of roaring dogs. They were going to enjoy the leavings of the feast too.

The mice ran for their lives and hid in a corner. They lay trembling, hardly daring to breathe. Not till everybody had gone away did they dare to creep out.

"Well, my dear," said the Country Mouse, "if this is city life, good-by. I'll go back to the country. I would rather have my moldy crusts and dry peas in my own quiet hole than feast like this in fear of my life."

Crusts eaten in peace are better than cakes eaten in fear.

The Goose That Laid the Golden Eggs

A Farmer had a gray goose which one day gave him a big surprise. In her nest he found a strange egg. It was as yellow as gold and very heavy.

"Somebody has been playing a joke on me," he thought at first. Then he realized that the egg was pure gold.

"Wife!" he shouted happily as soon as he got in the house. "See what our gray goose has laid—an egg of pure gold!"

What was the Farmer's joy when next day he found another golden egg in the nest! And the next day yet another.

It was wonderful! But by this time the Farmer had grown greedy. "Why should I wait?" he thought. "If I cut the goose open, I shall get all her golden eggs at once. My fortune will be made in a minute!"

So he killed the bird—but found not a single egg inside. And his good gray goose was dead.

He who is too greedy may end up with nothing.

The Frog and the Ox

"Oh, Mother!" cried three little Frogs to a big Frog. "We have just seen the most terrible monster! He was as big as a mountain and had horns on his head and a tail and hoofs."

"It was the Ox," said the mother. "He *is*

pretty tall, to be sure, but not much broader than I am. Just you wait and see."

And she began to huff and puff and blow herself out.

"Was the Ox bigger than that?" she asked.

"Oh, yes, Mother!" the little Frogs piped.

So the big Frog huffed and puffed some more and blew and blew herself out.

"Was he bigger than that?" she panted.

"Much, much bigger!"

The Frog took a still deeper breath. "Surely the Ox was no bigger than——" But she got no further. For here there was a "Pop!" and the Frog burst.

🖋 *Don't try to do what is impossible.*

The Miser

.16. There was once a man who loved money so much that he would not spend a penny if he could help it. All the Miser wanted to do was look at his money, and hold it in his hands, and gloat over it. At last he sold nearly every-thing he had and changed his money for a lump of gold. But then the Miser was afraid someone would steal it. So in the end he dug a hole by the wall of his garden and buried his lump of gold.

Every morning he would go to his wall, dig up his treasure, and look at it. Then he would bury it again.

One morning he went to his hiding place as usual. To his horror he saw that someone had been before him. The ground was all dug up. And the gold was gone.

"Thieves! thieves!" he cried. "I have been robbed!" And he began to weep and wail so loudly that his neighbor came running.

"Don't take it so hard," he comforted the Miser when he heard the story. "Nothing so terrible has happened to you. Just bury a stone there and pretend that it is gold. Since you never meant to spend it, a stone will be just as good as a lump of gold."

Money has no true value if it is not used.

The Old Lion and the Fox

A Lion grew so old that he could no longer hunt for his food. But old or not, he had to eat. So he thought up a plan. He would make believe he was sick. And when visitors came to see him, he would eat them up.

Well, things worked out just as he planned. He lay down near the mouth of his cave and began to groan. One after another the beasts came to ask him what was the matter. The Lion invited them in—and that was the end of them.

One day the Fox heard the Lion groaning. He came up and sat down outside the Lion's cave.

"Aren't you feeling well?" he asked.

"I am very sick, friend Fox," the Lion answered. "And it is so lonesome lying here by myself. Do come in and visit me for a little while."

"Well, I'd like to," answered the Fox. "But I see by the tracks around here that you've had quite a lot of visitors lately. Strangely, the tracks go only one way. They all point *towards* your cave. Until the animals that have gone in come out again, I'll stay in the fresh air, thank you."

The Lion had no answer for that. So with a laugh the Fox walked off.

Be warned by what happens to others.

The Fox and the Grapes

One fine fall day a Fox was running lightly through the woods when the cry of a bird made him look up. What should he see right over his head but a big bunch of purple grapes! They were wild but quite large and perfectly ripe.

The Fox licked his lips. "Grapes are just the thing for my thirst," he thought.

Now the grapevine had trailed itself over a high tree branch, and the bunch of grapes hung out of reach. "But they are worth leaping for," the Fox told himself.

So he leaped high with open mouth. Not

quite high enough, though, for his jaws snapped on empty air.

"Well, next time I shan't miss," he said. And he leaped again. Once more he came down with nothing to show for it.

"I'll try from the other side," he thought. He took a run, leaped, and—missed. Then he tried again. And again. A hundred times he jumped. All in vain.

At last he gave up, turned his back on the grapes, and went crossly on his way. "I am sure they are sour anyway," he said. "There wasn't a ripe grape among them."

It is easy to say something is no good if you cannot get it.

The Two Frogs

One August day two Frogs were hopping .21. along a dusty road. They were looking for water. All summer long there had been no rain and every pond around them had dried up.

At last to their joy the Frogs came upon a well. They hopped to the edge. Eagerly they looked down. Far, far below at the bottom they could see the glint of water.

"We have come to the end of our journey!" one of the Frogs said. And he got ready to dive in.

"Hold on!" the other Frog cried. "Let's think a minute. The reason this well has water in it is that it is very deep. Now supposing it, too, goes dry. Where will we be then? In a fine fix—no water and no way of getting out. Jump in if you have a mind to. But as for me, I'll hop along till I come to a stream."

Think twice before you leap.

The Miller, His Son, and the Donkey

.22.

A Miller and his Son set off for the market one day. They were going to sell their old Donkey.

"We won't ride him," the Miller said. "For it is a hot day. We want him to look fresh when we sell him."

So all three walked slowly along the road.

"What fools you are!" a passing farmer called out to them. "A Donkey is to ride, isn't it? Then why do you walk?" And he laughed merrily at them.

The Miller didn't like that. So he told his boy to climb up on the Donkey.

Pretty soon they met a pedlar pushing a cart.

"Aren't you ashamed of yourself?" the pedlar said to the boy. "Your legs are young and strong. You should let your father ride."

The Miller wasn't a bit tired. But he said, "Get down, Son." And they changed places.

They had not gone far when they passed some women going to the market with eggs to sell.

"What kind of a man are you?" one of the women scolded. "A big, strong fellow like you riding while his poor little boy has to walk!"

The Miller didn't know what to do now.

But at last he told his Son to get up behind him.

They were almost in sight of the town by this time, and many people were on the highway.

"Look at that Donkey!" the Miller heard one man say to another. "The poor creature can hardly walk. I call it cruel to overload a dumb animal that way."

"I agree," the other said. "Those two look more fit to carry the Donkey than he is to carry them."

The Miller and his Son both got down. The father stepped off the road and cut a long pole. To this they tied the Donkey's four feet. Then they put the pole on their shoulders. And there was the Donkey going to market upside down!

From all sides the people came running. Never had they seen such a sight as that. Some pitied the Miller and his Son. Some pitied the Donkey. But mostly they just shouted and laughed.

Meantime the Donkey was very unhappy. He didn't like being carried, and upside down at that. And he was upset by all the noise. He started to struggle and bray. Just as they stepped on Market Bridge, he got one of his feet loose. He kicked out at the boy, who dropped his end of the pole. The next minute the Donkey had rolled off the bridge into the water. And before anyone could fish him out, he drowned. For how could he swim with three feet still tied to the pole?

"I tried to please everybody," the Miller said as they set out sadly for home. "But I pleased nobody. And now my old Donkey is lost."

🐚 *If you try to please all, you will please none.*

Androcles and the Lion

There was once a slave called Androcles. His master was so cruel to him that at last Androcles ran away and hid in the forest.

One day he heard a moaning and a groaning close by. He crept up. And there was a Lion lying on the ground! Androcles was about to run away, but just then he saw that one of the Lion's paws was bleeding and badly swollen.

Now Androcles loved animals. He couldn't bear to see the Lion in pain. So he came still closer to see if he could help.

The Lion held up his swollen paw. It had a huge thorn in it.

"Hold on, old fellow!" Androcles said gently. "I'll get the nasty thorn out for you. But don't you bite me!"

The Lion roared with pain while Androcles drew out the thorn. But he didn't bite. And when it was all over, he licked the slave's hand. Then he limped away.

Soon after this both Androcles and the Lion were captured by Roman soldiers. And the Roman judges said that the runaway slave Androcles should be thrown to the Lion.

So they starved the Lion for three days. Then the whole city and the Emperor and all .27. his court came to see the Lion tear the runaway slave to pieces. They climbed up into their seats in the arena. Androcles was driven out into the center of the huge circle. And then the Lion was let out of his cage.

He came roaring toward Androcles. He got ready to spring. But suddenly he stopped. Making happy noises, he trotted over to Androcles. And what did the people see? The Lion licking the slave's hands and face!

Well, the end of it was that Androcles was set free. And the wonderful Lion was taken back to live happily in his forest.

A noble soul never forgets a kindness.

The Stag and His Reflection

A Stag stood looking at his reflection in a forest pool.

"How beautiful my antlers are!" he thought. "They are like many-branching trees. But my legs, now—they are nothing to be proud of. So thin and bony. And my knees——"

He didn't finish, for just then an arrow whistled close by him. The Stag sped through

the forest. Soon he was far away and almost out of danger. But then, as he plunged wildly through a thicket, his antlers were caught in it. A second arrow now whistled through the air. And this time it struck him down.

"How foolish I was to think ill of my legs!" the dying Stag thought. "My legs would have saved me. But my antlers, which I admired so much, have brought me to my death."

🖋 *We often think ill of what is most useful to us.*

The Lark and Her Young Ones

A Lark had built her nest in a wheat field. When the wheat was ripe, the Lark knew that she and her family would soon have to move.

"Keep your ears open," she told her Young Ones before she flew off to get food for them.

"See if you can learn when the wheat will be cut. For we have to leave before that happens."

By the time the Lark came back, the Young Ones had news for her.

"The farmer and his son were here!" they cried. "They are going to call their neighbors to help them cut the wheat. We'd better leave!"

"No hurry, no hurry," their mother said.

The next day while she was getting food, the Young Ones saw the farmer and his son again.

"Oh, Mother," they said when the Lark returned, "the farmer is going to ask his friends to help cut the wheat. Let's move right away."

"No hurry yet, my dears," the Lark said.

The next day the young birds had news again. "The farmer was here, Mother. He told his boy the grain is so ripe that it will fall to the ground. If he doesn't cut it, he will lose it, he said. So tomorrow he is coming to cut the wheat himself."

"Now it is indeed time to go," the Lark said. "For now the wheat will really be cut. When a man does not depend on anyone to help him, the job will get done."

.31.

If you want something to be surely done, do it yourself.

The Grasshopper and the Ant

All summer long the Grasshopper could be heard in the fields. He hopped and he leaped and he sang away at the top of his voice. "The sun is warm!" he sang. "The leaves taste good! It is so nice to be alive!"

The summer days passed quickly. It seemed to the Hopper he had barely turned around when already it was fall. The cold wind was blowing. All the flowers and grasses in the field were dead. The bushes and the trees had stripped themselves for their winter sleep. And there was nothing to eat—simply nothing.

The Grasshopper no longer sang about how nice it was to be alive. Indeed, how could he live at all if somebody didn't help him?

"Please," he said, stumbling over to an Ant, "will you give me something to eat?"

The Ant was busy. She was dragging a dead fly into the nest. It was one of a hundred insects she had lugged home. For she had worked, worked, worked all summer, storing up food for the winter.

She stopped a moment to stare at the beggar.

"Something to eat?" she asked sternly. "And what, if you please, were you doing all summer? That is the time when sensible folk provide for the winter."

"I had no time to work," the Grasshopper said. "Please don't be cross with me. All summer long I hopped and leaped and sang."

"What? All you did was sing and prance?" cried the Ant, turning her back on him. "Well, my good fellow, now you can dance!"

🖋 *Prepare today for the needs of tomorrow.*

The Hare and the Tortoise

The Hare was showing off before the other animals.

"I can run faster than any of you," he boasted. "Nobody can beat me."

"Well, I'm not so sure of that," a low voice said. "I'll race you if you like."

It was the Tortoise speaking. Everybody was

surprised, for they all knew what a slowpoke he was.

The Hare laughed. "That's a good joke," he said.

"But I mean it," the Tortoise said. "Let's have a race."

So the animals marked out a race course. The runners would start here on the dirt road, and they would end there, by the big oak tree.

"It's a good two miles," said the Hare. "Now let's go!" And at the word of command he started lickety-split down the road.

In half a minute the Hare was almost out of sight. He looked back. The Tortoise had moved only a couple of yards!

"I've got plenty of time to take a nap," the Hare said to himself with a grin. And just to make fun of the Tortoise, he lay down and made believe he had gone to sleep. But it was a hot day, and before he knew it he really was asleep.

By and by he woke up with a start. Wasn't he supposed to be in a race with somebody? He looked back down the road. Nobody there.

He looked the other way. There was the Tortoise—almost at the end of the course!

The Hare laid his ears back close to his body and dashed away at his highest speed. But it was too late. Before he could get to the oak tree, the Tortoise was already there, resting quietly in its shade.

🖋 *Slow and sure is better than fast and careless.*

The Fox without a Tail

A Fox once had his tail caught in a trap.

"My life is worth more than my tail," he said. So he pulled and jerked and yanked till he tore himself out of the trap. But he had to leave his bushy tail behind him.

Now a Fox's tail is his chief claim to beauty. So the Fox was ashamed even to show himself among the other foxes. He was just sick over the loss of his tail.

"All my life," he thought, "I shall be the only Fox without a tail. That's how others will speak of me. They will call me The Fox Without A Tail. If only it would become the fashion for foxes to have no tails! Then I should at least be in style."

At last he decided on a bold plan. He called a meeting of the foxes. And he spoke to them as follows:

"Brothers," he said, "I want to bring up a subject that has long been on my mind. Why should we foxes have tails? Tails are nothing but a trouble to us. So heavy to carry around! Always in the way when we want to sit down! We can't use them for anything. And isn't it for the sake of our tails that we are hunted? We could get away from the dogs much faster if we didn't have to carry our tails. So I propose," he ended, "that all foxes cut off their tails."

He spoke and backed away into the shadows.

An old Fox got up then. "My friend," he said, "come forward again and kindly turn around. Let all the foxes see why you want us to cut off our tails. You wouldn't ask us to do

it if you had any chance of getting your own
tail back again."

🐿 *Before you take advice, be sure it is given for*
your sake.

The Monkey and the Cat

A Monkey and a Cat were pets in the same
house. They were great friends and were
always doing something naughty together.

One day they were sitting in front of a fire,
watching some chestnuts roasting.

"How nice it would be to have some chestnuts," the Monkey said. "You are so clever at
such things, Kitty! Much more clever than I
am. Pull some chestnuts out of the fire and I
will divide them between us."

The Cat didn't like to put her paw so close
to the flames. But she was flattered by what
the Monkey had said about her. So she put
out her paw and very carefully drew out a
chestnut. Though she burned her paw each

time, she did the trick again and again. But as fast as she pulled the chestnuts out of the fire, the Monkey gobbled them up.

"What are you two naughty ones up to now?" their little mistress scolded, coming into the room.

The Monkey and the Cat scampered away. The Cat was feeling her burns at every step. "Next time, friend Monkey," she said as she sat down to lick her paw, "I'll know better. I'll not pull chestnuts out of the fire for you again."

Watch out! The flatterer always wants to get something out of you.

The Jackdaw
and His Borrowed Feathers

.40. A Jackdaw flew over the wall into a garden where peacocks walked. No one was around. But there on the ground lay some beautiful peacock plumes. Quickly he gathered them up.

"How fine I will look dressed up in these peacock feathers!" he thought.

He stuck the longest ones in his tail and some of the shorter ones on his head. Then he flew back among the crows and starlings and sparrows. He strutted around proudly. He made believe he didn't even see the common birds.

"I really am too fine to talk to them," he decided at last, and flew off to the peacocks. But the peacocks saw at once that he was a Jackdaw dressed in their feathers. They came up angrily and pecked their plumes off him. And along with the borrowed feathers, the Jackdaw lost some of his own.

It was a sad-looking bird that flew back over the wall. He was glad to get away with both eyes in his head. Now he was ready to be friends with the common birds around him. But the starlings and crows and sparrows remembered what airs he had put on before. And they would have nothing to do with him.

.41.

Borrowed feathers do not make fine birds.

Two Fellows and a Bear

Two young men were traveling together through a wood. Suddenly they heard a crashing noise near them.

"Great heavens, it's a Bear!" cried the one who was in the lead. He thought of nothing but saving himself. And taking hold of a low branch, he swung himself up into the nearest tree.

The other Traveler had no time to get away. Left alone, he flung himself down with his face to the ground and held his breath. He made believe he was dead. For he had heard that a Bear will not eat a dead body.

The Bear walked over. He sniffed all around and even put his muzzle close to the Traveler's ear. Then, with a low growl, he went off about his business.

The "dead" man sat up. His companion came down from his tree.

"That Bear looked just as if he was whispering to you," he said, laughing. "What did he say to you?"

"He advised me," the other man said, "to

get a better fellow to travel with. For one who leaves his friend in a pinch is a coward."

🖋 *It is a poor friend who deserts you when you are in trouble.*

The Travelers and the Purse

Two men were traveling together along a road. Suddenly one of them stooped and picked up a purse. Someone had lost it on the way.

"Look what I have found!" he cried. "It is very heavy. It must be full of money."

Quickly he opened it. "How lucky I am!" he said when he saw that it was full of gold.

"You should say how lucky *we* are," his companion said. "Aren't we traveling together? Travelers should share both their good luck and their bad."

"No, indeed!" the other said. "*I* found it and *I* am going to keep it!"

He had no sooner said this than they heard

a cry of "Stop, thief!" They looked behind them. A mob of people was streaming toward them. And everyone in that mob was armed with a heavy stick.

The Traveler who had picked up the purse grew pale with fright.

"We are lost if they find the purse upon us!" he cried. "They will think we stole it!"

But his companion did not share his fright. "Don't say *we* are lost," he said. "You would not say *we* before. So now say *I* am lost."

If you do not share your good fortune with others, don't expect them to share in your misfortunes.

The Frog and the Mouse

A young Mouse was running along the edge of a pond. He was looking for adventure.

"So you have come to see what my watery world is like," said a Frog. And he swam up to the Mouse. "Come! I will show it to you."

The Mouse was very willing. "But I can't swim very well," he said. "Will you help me?"

"Easiest thing in the world," said the Frog. "All we need do is tie your leg to one of mine with a reed."

The foolish Mouse let the Frog do just that. But when the Frog jumped into the pond and dragged him along to the bottom, the Mouse didn't like it at all.

"Let me go!" he screamed. "I can't breathe! I will drown!"

The hard-hearted Frog, however, would not listen. And the Mouse ended his adventure by losing his life.

Did the Frog care? No! But something evil was in store for him, too. Before he could untie the dead Mouse from his leg, a hawk came sailing over the water. He spotted the Mouse from on high. Down he swooped, picked it up in his claws, and carried it off. And the Frog willy-nilly had to go along too.

He who plots to harm another often comes to harm himself.

The Wind and the Sun

The Wind boasted to the Sun one day: "I am stronger than you by far. Just see how the dead leaves whirl and flee before me!"

The Sun smiled. "You are mistaken," he said quietly.

"Let's see you prove it!" the Wind snapped back.

Just then a traveler came down the road.

"I think I see a way of proving it," the Sun said. "See that traveler down there? Let us agree that he who can make him take off his cloak is the stronger. You may have your turn first."

So the Sun went behind a cloud, and the Wind started to blow. The traveler's cloak flapped wildly. But the harder the Wind tried to tear off the cloak, the more tightly the man drew it around him.

At last the Wind gave up. "Go ahead! Have your try at it," he said.

Smiling, the Sun came out from behind the cloud. He shone in all his glory, pouring his warm beams on the traveler.

"How hot it has suddenly grown!" the traveler said. And he took off his cloak.

Kindness is better than force.

The Ant and the Dove

A thirsty Ant was climbing down a blade of grass that grew beside a spring. He was trying to reach the water so he could take a drink. Unluckily he slipped and tumbled into the spring.

Now a Dove was sitting on a branch over the water. She saw the Ant fall in and was struck with pity. Quick as a wink she plucked off a leaf and let it fall into the spring. The little raft settled down on the water right beside the drowning Ant. The insect climbed aboard and was soon safe on shore again.

But what did he see? Hidden behind a bush, a hunter was spreading his net. He was going to snare the Dove!

"No, indeed!" the grateful Ant said. "You

.49.

shall not take the bird that saved my life!" And with all his force he stung the hunter on his bare heel.

With a cry the hunter dropped his net. Next moment the startled Dove was flying away to the wood.

One good turn deserves another.

The Mice in Trouble

"It is terrible! Just terrible! We really must do something about it! But what?"

The Mice were talking about the Cat. One by one they were falling into her claws. She would steal up softly, softly on her pussy feet. Then suddenly she would spring—and there was one mouse less.

At last the Mice held a meeting to decide what to do. One said this, another said that. But mostly they spoke about how terrible and sad things were. Nobody had any plan.

Then a young mouse jumped up. "I know

what we should do!" he said brightly. "Tie a bell around the Cat's neck! Then we would hear her coming and we would run away fast!"

The Mice clapped their little paws for joy. What a good idea! Why hadn't they thought of it before? And what a very clever little fellow this young mouse was!

But now a very old mouse, who hadn't opened his mouth all this time, got up to speak.

"Friends," he said, "I agree that the plan of the young mouse is very clever indeed. But I should like to ask one question: Which of us is going to tie the bell around the Cat's neck?"

There is no use offering a plan that cannot be carried out.

The Fox and the Crow

One morning a Crow got hold of a piece of cheese.

"What luck!" she thought, and flew up on a dead branch to enjoy it.

Now a Fox was just then passing the spot. At the sharp smell of cheese he stopped dead in his tracks and sniffed all around the tree. Then he looked up. There sat the Crow with the cheese in her beak.

"How nice it would be to start my breakfast with a piece of cheese!" thought the Fox.

His mouth watered for the tidbit. But he couldn't climb up and take the cheese away, for Foxes don't climb trees. And anyway the Crow would fly off before he got there. "No, my wits will have to get the cheese for me," he said to himself. And in his friendliest tone he called out to the Crow:

"Good morning!"

The Crow knew better than to answer. If she opened her mouth, she would drop the cheese. So she just sat and listened.

"My dear," the Fox went on, "how lovely you are! Your eyes are so bright, your tail is so perky! Your plumes shine like the morning sun. Tell me, Beautiful Creature, can you also

sing? Now don't be bashful. Just let me hear you. If your voice matches the rest of your charms, I will say you are the finest bird in these woods."

Up on her dead branch the Crow was dizzy with joy. Nobody had ever said such wonderful things to her before. She wanted very much to show the Fox that she could also sing. So she opened her beak and gave out a loud, harsh "Caw."

That was all the Fox was waiting for. He snapped up the cheese even before it reached the ground.

"I'll give you a piece of advice," he said as he turned to go. "Don't let flattery make a fool of you!"

🖋 *Take care! Flattery works—more or less—on nearly all of us.*

· 54 ·

The Shepherd Boy

A young Shepherd Boy pastured his sheep beside a deep, dark forest. It was a pleasant enough job. He could sit on a rock and play his pipe. He could lie on his back and watch the white clouds sailing while the sheep grazed around him. But it was too quiet and peaceful for him. He wanted excitement. So one day he decided to play a trick.

"Wolf! Wolf!" he shouted in his loudest voice.

In the still air his cry carried far. The farmers working in the fields heard him. "A Wolf is after our sheep!" they called out to one another. One seized a pitchfork, another an ax, a third his spade. And they ran to the meadow to kill the Wolf.

But when they got there, no Wolf was to be seen. The sheep were quietly grazing, and the Shepherd Boy was dancing around in glee. "I fooled you! I fooled every one of you!" he shouted.

A few days later the Shepherd Boy played the same trick. And once more the farmers came running for nothing.

But the very next day a Wolf really did come out of the forest and fall on the sheep.

"Wolf! Wolf!" the Shepherd Boy shouted at the top of his lungs. Again and again he called, "Wolf! Wolf!" The sound rolled down to the busy farmers in their fields.

But no one came to his help. "He is playing his tricks on us again," the farmers said and kept on working.

So the Wolf feasted well that day and killed many sheep.

🗡 *A liar will not be believed even when he tells the truth.*

The Wolf and the Lamb

A young Lamb strayed from the flock one hot summer day. How glad he was to find a sparkling brook! He walked right into the water, bent his woolly head down, and began to drink. He never noticed that a Wolf was drinking from the same stream. But the Wolf saw him.

"What a fine dinner has come to me!" he

thought. "And without the least trouble on my part!"

Yet the Lamb looked so harmless that the Wolf wanted a reason for eating him. So he growled and said:

"How dare you muddy the water I drink?"

All in a tremble the Lamb looked up. There stood the wicked enemy just a few steps away!

"Your Highness," he answered softly, "how can I muddy your drink? If your Honor will look, you will see that the stream flows downhill from where you stand to me."

"So you call me a liar?" shouted the Wolf. "You bold, bad creature! Meanness is written all over your face! And now I remember that last year you spread tales about me."

"Your Highness, I couldn't have done that," the Lamb defended himself. "I was only born this spring."

"Well, if it wasn't you, it was your brother!" the Wolf snapped back.

"But I have no brother."

"Be silent!" The Wolf was in a rage now. "Then it was some other relative of yours," he roared. "All you sheep are our enemies. You and your shepherds and dogs have harmed us countless times. But I am going to settle with you this moment for all their crimes!"

"But, Sir!" pleaded the Lamb. "How am I to blame?"

"Be silent, I say! I am tired of hearing your silly excuses. Too much time has been spent in talk already. But if you want a reason, I'll give you one. You are to blame because I WANT TO EAT!"

And with that he leaped upon the Lamb.

The wicked will always find an excuse for doing what they like.

The Dog and His Shadow

Curly the Dog was happily trotting home. It wasn't every day that the butcher gave him a juicy bone with meat on it! The Dog was carrying it very carefully in his mouth.

On the way he had to cross a little stream.

He looked down from the footbridge into the clear water. And, to his surprise, he saw another dog under the water. Yes, and that other dog also had a bone in his mouth! It seemed to Curly that it was a bigger bone than his own.

With a growl he dropped his bone in order to grab the other dog's bone too. But he had no sooner done that than the dog under the water also dropped his bone.

For a moment Curly stood looking angrily down at his shadow. He couldn't understand it. All he knew was that he had lost his bone and must now trot home without it.

Grasp for all and lose all.

The Lion's Share

A Lion, a Fox, a Jackal, and a Wolf were neighbors once. The hunting was poor that fall and quite often one or another of the animals went hungry. One day the Lion called them together.

"Let us act like friends as well as neighbors," he said. "Let us share. Whatever one of us catches we will divide fairly among the four of us. That way we will all dine every day."

The rest agreed, and off they went to hunt, each after his own fashion.

That same morning the Fox had the good luck to kill a deer. Proudly he called the rest, and they came running.

"Not bad at all," they said, looking over the prey. They could hardly wait to sit down to the feast.

But first the deer had to be divided, and the Lion took charge of that.

"Neighbors," he said, "there are four of us." With this he tore the deer into quarters.

Then he put his paw on one of the quarters and said: "This part is mine. Our plan says so."

Next he drew another quarter towards him. "And this part is mine," he said, "because I am a Lion."

No one spoke; so he reached out and grabbed the third part too. "And this part is mine," he said, "because I am stronger and my reach is longer. And as for this last part— —" The Lion stopped to glare at each of the beasts in turn. "If one of you so much as dares to move a finger toward it, I promise he will not leave this place alive!"

So the Fox, the Jackal, and the Wolf sat and licked their chops while the Lion had a fine meal.

The law of the mighty is: Might makes right.

The Bundle of Sticks

There was once a man who had four sons. The Father loved them very much, but they troubled him greatly. For they were always fighting with one another. Nothing the Father said did any good.

"What can I do to show my boys how .62. wrong it is to act this way?" the Father thought.

One day he called the boys to him and showed them a bundle of sticks.

"Which of you, my sons, can break this bundle of sticks?" he asked them.

All the boys tried in turn, but not one of them could do it.

Then the Father untied the bundle and gave each boy a single stick. "See if you can break that," he said.

Of course, they could easily do it.

"My sons," the Father said, "each of you alone is weak. He is as easy to injure as one of these sticks. But if you will be friends and stick together, you will be as strong as the bundle of sticks."

When people stand together, they are strong.

The Boy and the Nuts

A Boy who was very fond of nuts was told one day that he could have a handful.

"As big a handful as I like?" he asked.

"As big a handful as you can take," his mother answered.

The Boy at once put his hand into the pitcher of nuts and grasped all his fist would hold. But when he tried to get his hand out, he found he couldn't because the neck of the pitcher was too narrow. He tried and tried to squeeze his hand through. At last he burst into tears. There he stood crying, yet unwilling to let a single nut go.

"The fault is not with the pitcher, my Boy," his mother said. "It is your greed that makes you cry. Be satisfied with half as many nuts and you will be able to get your hand out."

Half a loaf is better than none.

The Cat and the Fox

A Cat and a Fox were off on a trip together. They got on very well, but one day the Fox started boasting.

"I am far more clever than you," he said. "Why, I have a whole bagful of tricks."

"That may be," replied the Cat. "I admit

that I have only one trick. But I am willing to bet that it is worth a dozen of yours."

Just as he said this, a hunting horn sounded close by, and a pack of hunting dogs came over the hill.

The Cat at once ran up a tree. "This is my trick," he called down to the Fox. "Now let's see yours."

The Fox had so many plans of escape that he didn't know which to choose. So he tried one after another. He ran in zigzags. He doubled back on his tracks. He ran into one end of a hollow log and out at the other. He dived into burrow after burrow. But the dogs saw through all his tricks. They kept right at his heels. And at last they caught him.

One sure plan is worth a dozen that aren't.

.66.

The Eagle and the Crow

A young Crow was sitting on a rock beside a flock of sheep. Suddenly he saw an Eagle swoop down from the sky. The great bird picked up a lamb in his claws and carried it off to his nest.

"What's so hard about that?" the Crow thought. "I can do the same thing."

With that he flew up high, looked the flock over, and made his choice.

But what did he choose?

A ram. And what a ram! One with sides so fat, and fleece so thick, and horns so big that a wolf couldn't lift a load like that. The silly Crow dug his claws into the wool and pulled. He couldn't even stir the ram from the ground. Indeed, the ram hardly felt the bird on his back.

When the Crow saw he had made a mistake, he tried to fly away. But his claws were so tangled in the wool that he couldn't get them out. He flapped and flapped his wings, but could not free himself. He was a prisoner!

"Ho! what have we here?" the shepherd cried, running up. "A Crow! So you think you're an Eagle, do you? Well, we'll soon fix that!"

The Crow cawed his loudest, but it didn't help. The shepherd took him off the ram, clipped his wings, and gave him to the children for a pet.

🖋 *Know yourself! Do not undertake to do more than you are able.*

The Heron

A Heron was stalking along the bank of a stream early one morning. His eyes were fastened on the shallow water at the edge. For he hadn't eaten yet. He was waiting for something really worth-while to swim by.

"I'll not take any of your small fry," he said to himself. "My breakfast must be fit for a king."

As he watched, a fine perch swam by. But the Heron turned up his bill at it. "Not big enough," he said.

Then a catfish swam by.

"Too bony," the Heron said.

And so it went. Nothing was good enough. Something was wrong with every fish that came by.

But now the sun was higher in the sky. The fish left the shallow water and swam out into the deep, cool center of the stream. It was too deep there for the Heron to follow. He fussed and fussed. He hoped and hoped. But no more fish came by. Not even a tiny minnow. And at last, being very hungry, he was glad to breakfast on a little snail.

He who is hard to please may get very little in the end.

The Wolf and the Crane

Wolves are greedy. They eat so fast they don't know what is meat and what is bone. And that is how one of them nearly lost his life.

He choked on a bone, which stuck deep in his throat. The Wolf could hardly breathe and couldn't groan at all. He tried every way he knew to get the bone either up or down. He rolled on the ground and stretched his neck. He stood on his head. But nothing worked. The bone wouldn't shift from its position. And in despair he thought, "My time has come to die."

Luckily a Crane chanced to pass that way. The Wolf quickly pointed to his throat and then to her beak and showed very clearly by his signs what he wanted the Crane to do. She didn't like the idea at all. Who would? Who would trust his head in a Wolf's mouth? But the Crane was greedy and thought, "He will reward me handsomely for saving his life."

So she stuck her long beak deep down in the Wolf's throat, got hold of the bone, and pulled it out.

"There," she said, laying it on the ground. "The bone you choked on lies before you. And now, Sir, pay me for my trouble."

"You are joking!" cried the Wolf. "Didn't you get your pay already? You had your head in my mouth and I didn't snap it off. Get out of my sight, you stupid thing! And in future see that you don't cross my path!"

🖋 *If you serve the wicked, don't expect any reward.*

The Wolf and the Goat

A Wolf had no luck in his hunting one day. Late in the afternoon he was passing by a cliff when he saw a Goat grazing on its very top. The Goat saw the Wolf too. But he wasn't afraid. He knew he was quite safe up there on the steep cliff.

The hungry Wolf thought to himself: "I must say something to make that Goat come down so I can get him for my dinner." And clearing his throat, he began to speak in his softest voice.

"O Goat!" he called out. "I wouldn't stay up there if I were you. It's not safe. You might easily fall. Think how sad it would be if you broke a leg. You'd better come down here.

There is lots of fresh green grass here where I am sitting. I think you'll not find better grass than this in the whole land."

But the Goat was too old to be tricked. "That Wolf wants my life," he thought. And looking over the edge of the cliff, he said, "Thank you, friend. You are very kind to look after me this way. And it is so good of you to offer me your grass. But I know you a little too well to be fooled. It is not of my dinner you are thinking, good Sir, but of your own!"

Look to see what lies behind an invitation.

The Fox and the Goat

One day a Fox was nosing around a well. By bad luck his foot slipped on a wet stone and he fell in. The water wasn't deep, but the well was. And though he wore himself out trying to get out, the Fox could not do it.

"What in the world are you doing down there in the well?" he heard someone ask. He

looked up. There stood a Goat peering down in the well.

The Fox's spirits rose. He saw hope ahead.

"Enjoying myself!" he replied. "They say there will be no rain for a long time and all the wells will go dry. So I am drinking my fill before it happens. Come on down—the water's fine."

The foolish Goat didn't stop to think. He jumped right in.

The Fox, of course, wanted to use him for a ladder and leaped at once on the Goat's back. Then he set one foot on his horns and jumped out of the well.

"Good-by, my friend," he called out from above. "And next time, silly Goat, look before you leap!"

Think how you will get out before you get in.

The Wolf and the House Dog

One day a Wolf met a House Dog on the highway. The Wolf was lean with hunger while the Dog was in fine shape. Indeed, if the Dog had not looked quite so husky, the Wolf would have tried to eat him.

"You certainly are just skin and bones," the Dog said with pity. "That, my friend, is because you don't eat regularly. Now I do. For breakfast——" And he went on to tell about all the good things he ate every day of his life and the extras on holidays.

"That is the secret of health," he ended. "Keep thieves away from the master's house and have your food given to you regularly."

"I wouldn't mind that," the Wolf said.

"Then come with me," the Dog invited.

So they went on toward the town. But all at once the Wolf noticed something. In one place around the Dog's neck the hair was worn away.

"How did that happen?" the Wolf asked.

"That? Oh, that's nothing," the Dog said. "That's the place where the collar is put on when they chain me up. It chafes a bit."

"What?" cried the Wolf. He stopped dead in his tracks. "Do you mean to say you are not always free to come and go as you please?"

"Well, not all the time," said the Dog.

"Then good-by, my friend," the Wolf said. And back he ran to the forest.

🖌 *It is better to starve and be free than to eat well and be a slave.*